# The
# CLIFF EDGE

## By

## Ray Kohn

For

**Pat**

# CONTENTS

# Copyrights

All these stories are my own: no one else is responsible for textual errors, poor narrative or bad taste. First: important friends: quiet support from Graham Roos in Sheffield and Gerry Gillespie in Cyprus has helped me more than they know. Second: Members of the Sheffield Authors group who have encouraged me include Carmel Page, Steve Kay, Berlie Doherty and Bill Allerton. Without Bill's assistance I would never have managed to have these stories published. Without my wife's patient support, I would probably never have written at all.

# FASHION SHOWS

The sole cultural activity inherited from the Mammalian Era was the fashion show. The competition between trees aspiring to be recognised as the way forward in the Mycelian Era was intense. In the millennial evolution during which the trees were encouraged into mobility by the mushroom intelligentsia, the beauty of the Beech had been celebrated in every corner of the civilised world. But the international fashion show held every ten years threatened a closer competition as the advances made by the Firs and Oaks had been telegraphed through the Mycelian subterranean network, deliberately challenging the Beech's presumption of supremacy.

The failure of the giant Redwood to have evolved beyond giantism had been one of the most disappointing aspects of the fashion industry. Others who just shaved off leaves failed to approach the slender elegance of the Beeches – the yardstick by which judgements were made. Ash design schools had grown as an advisory educational infrastructure whose objectivity was respected as Ashes never took part in competition. But Ash leaders were unimpressed by the arrogance displayed by Beeches who could not envisage any serious contenders to displace their leading models.

Entry into the competition was a two-stage process enabling judges to cut out poor performers in round one. Traditionally, this is when the little bushes were thanked for their efforts but excluded from the embarrassment of appearing to the worldwide audience in the final round. The rules, however, did permit a new entrant at round two provided the tree traversed more than one continent.

So, in the fateful year dominated by the Poplar late entrant, it was not only fellow arboreal competitors who were shocked by what was revealed. Taking the contemporary shaved look to its logical conclusion astonished the judges when the Poplars appeared stark naked! The daringly erect branches could be viewed without any leafy covering. Mycelian judges were divided as never before. Some were appalled at the temerity of the entrant whilst the Ashes, seeking innovation beyond Beech presumption of superiority, were moved by the audacity and curvaceous beauty of what all could see.

The disqualification of the Poplars by the mycelian arbiters who ruled that full coverage of more than one continent could not be proved failed to moderate the impact that the foliage-free Poplars made. The fashion for shedding leaves even before they had had the chance to develop each Spring saw almost every species of tree attempting to outdo one another in the smoothness of their bark, the shapeliness of their branches and the innocence of their pretty twigs and buds.

Mycelian screams at the dangers were ignored as photosynthetic activity virtually ceased. The gaunt and dying arboreal nudes inadvertently starved the underground mycelian network of the energy essential for its survival. Without informed leadership from below, leaflessness across all continents became the norm. And by the time even the most thoughtless tree had realised the danger, it was too late to avert the catastrophe as most trees had long forgotten how to generate their traditional Springtime covering. The fashion passion for sapling appearance had devastating consequences.

With insufficient oxygen generation as forest neighbours tried to outdo each other in how much bare bark they could show, the planet's atmosphere had a spike in carbon dioxide. The resulting trapped and heated air melted the polar ice caps and raised the oceans to levels not seen since the demise of the Mammalian Era. Outcrops of surviving islands where Mycelian soil retained integrity were only possible by the grim refusal of the local Beeches to strip.

The Cetacean Era has now lasted longer and been more peaceful than any period in Earth's history. Fortunately, dolphins, porpoises and whales see no benefit in competing in an aquatic fashion show.

# SON OF A GUN

"That is the worst idea I've heard in years. Don't your research team ever think about anything except appearances? The company needs genuine innovation. We require breakthrough products that generate new markets. Sticking a shiny, secondary barrel on our self-loading rifle just does not make the investment in your team worthwhile."

Research Director Kravitsky had heard all this before. Whenever his CEO was presented with something he didn't understand, he would go off on one of his standard speeches about whether research teams were worth the money allocated to them. Myers, the deputy CEO, was standing beside him. Kravitsky found Myers far more receptive and intelligent than his boss. But it was the CEO who made all the decisions about funding, and he always seemed to enjoy showing off his powers to Myers.

"We realise that nothing would do unless it was genuinely innovatory," Kravitsky replied. "But I am sure you would appreciate a red-hot demonstration of what this can achieve. I know you've read the brief, but would you care to accompany me to the range downstairs and see what we call the son of a gun in action?"

Grumbling about how much time is wasted in ascending and descending within the Alpha Omega Building, the CEO and Myers followed Kravitsky into the hyper-lift. Without any cables or old-fashioned elevator technology, they arrived at the range in less than five seconds.

"OK. I'm here. Now show me why I should fund this additional gun barrel."

"Well, sir, the son of a gun might look like a barrel, but it isn't. It's more like a sight setter. And it is ready to use."

"Good God! We have some of the most elegantly beautiful, laser-guided sights in our armoury. What is so special about this clumsy-looking thing?"

"If you look at the other end of the range, you will see that we have set up half a dozen targets. To make the test easier, we have coloured each of them differently. If you would care to hold the rifle. You do not need to aim it anywhere. Just hold it so the barrel is not facing you."

"I should bloody well hope not!"

"Actually, it would probably work even if it was facing you: but let's not take any risks. Just look at one of the targets that you want to hit. Then press the secondary barrel's rocker switch and the rifle will shoot your chosen target. It will hit it every time."

The CEO looked at Myers and then at Kravitsky. Myers and he were aware of the Research Director's notorious tricks. If this was another one, he did not think it was very funny. He had probably already used neurolinguistic programming to ensure that he would choose one of the targets. He reflected on the words that Kravitsky had used: he knew how this worked. He remembered how the man had described the demonstration as "red-hot". He said he assumed he had "read" the brief (of course he hadn't) and he had gone on to say it was "ready". He was clearly being preprogrammed to select the red target. Of course, the red target would already have explosives embedded so that it would appear this new barrel had almost magical powers. He held the rifle up pointing at the roof, looked straight at the blue target and pressed the rocker switch.

The blue target exploded as it was struck by the

incendiary bullet.

"How do you think he pulled off that trick?" the CEO asked Myers.

Myers answered. "Well, sir, I am not certain how it works but I would certainly want to fund the follow-up development program."

The CEO was annoyed at this easy cave-in to Kravitsky's demonstration. He did not know how he had achieved this illusion: but he certainly was not going to fall for it.

"I do not know what sleight of hand or conjuror's trick you have played on me, but I am not as easily fooled as Myers here. You may have pre-programmed me somehow: but you did not know Myers would be here. So, let's see if he can use the second barrel to hit a target. Let him have the rifle."

Kravitsky gingerly handed it over to the deputy. Myers concentrated on the target and fired.

CEO Myers now provides all the resources required to develop the 'son of a gun'.

# THE CLIFF EDGE

The moment had arrived. There was no turning back. The young couple had been pursued by Gregory's men all day. Gregory knew that Sam and Sandy had evaded capture dozens of times. But now he had them in his sights. There was surely no escape as they ran towards the cliff edge.

"Do you think we should jump?" Sandy asked.

Sam nodded. "They have their dogs. They can sniff us out. We can't outrun them along the parapet. I don't think we'll have any choice."

"If we leap from here, we might just about reach the water."

"We'd need to jump away from the cliff to avoid landing on the rocks."

The sound of the barking dogs suddenly seemed much nearer. Sandy wrapped her arms around Sam and said: "If we don't make it, you must know I love you."

Sam kissed Sandy and hugged her in his strong arms.

The first dog raced towards them, having been released from its lead. Sam glanced behind and, holding Sandy tight, ran towards the cliff edge. They grasped each other's hands, and, without a moment's hesitation, both leapt out into the shimmering air as it rose from the rocks, heated by the tropical sun.

Graham closed the book. "What happened next dad?"

"You'll have to wait for tomorrow night for the next instalment" he replied, as he tucked up his pre-school twins in bed.

Graham's problem with his boys was their insatiable appetite for adventure stories. He had already read his own books and had exhausted all the local reading library had to offer. Now, to satisfy the kids, he sat beside them with any book – tonight it was the railway timetable – pretending to read the latest adventure. But his capacity for invention was coming to an end. He was not sure he had any more stories inside him.

Downstairs, Barbara, his wife asked if the boys were asleep.

"I doubt it. They are probably thinking about how Sam and Sandy are going to escape."

"Who are Sam and Sandy?"

"That's a very good question, my love. I wonder if you would like to take over the storytelling tomorrow night. Then I could ask you what happened to them after they jumped off the cliff."

The tv was showing an old show that Graham had seen dozens of times. He yawned so Barbara switched off the television saying, "You are tired. Let's get ready for bed."

Barbara fell asleep in minutes, but Graham could not rest. What was he going to tell the children tomorrow? He had left Sam and Sandy suspended in midair. The kids would want to know what happened next. He considered the options. They could suddenly grow magic wings or be rescued by an alien spacecraft: but he remembered how dismissive both the kids were when he had created a science fiction scenario. They could fail to clear the rocks, be smashed to death so that he would not need to invent any alternative ending: but the pair were so sensitive that this would give them nightmares for the rest of the week. Graham dozed off, dreaming he was fast approaching a cliff edge. He awoke with a start, gripping the sheets to avoid an imagined fall.

His work colleague, Ray, had evolved a clever solution to a similar problem with his kids. He had invented a small set of imaginary characters who returned, again and again, in every story, enjoying parties (demonstrating good humour), travel (with incidental geography lessons included) and other nonsense that Ray's children loved to imagine. He had tried this with his two only to be told, in no uncertain terms, that "we have already heard about them: we want a new story."

Graham went to work the next day, tired. In his imagination, the approaching cliff face loomed larger as the day progressed. He told Ray about his dilemma, but his friend was not sympathetic. "Kids cannot expect eternal novelty. It's like families where the child expects a new toy every week until the house gets crammed with all that infantile paraphernalia!" Graham knew Ray was right but felt trapped by the excitement and expectation generated by his imaginative children.

Once home, the children were wide-eyed as they demanded to know if Sam and Sandy were going to be alright.

"You'll have to wait until bedtime before you can find out."

Barbara smiled, believing he was cleverly providing a means to persuade the kids to go quickly to bed when sent. The truth was that it just gave him more time to think as the cliff face approached.

"Daddy, we're in bed. Now please tell us what happens next."

Graham sat on the chair beside the bunk beds. He knew that there was no escape. He wondered whether real authors ever had the same experience – leaping into the dark, not knowing what was going to happen next in their stories. The cliff edge was a scary place.

"Come on daddy, stop thinking. Read us the rest of the story!"

Graham hesitated, nervously opening and shutting the railway timetable. "What do you think happens next?" he asked.

"Don't be silly, Daddy. It's your story. Tell us what really happens."

That was a strange idea … it was his story so him telling it made it "real"!

"I just wondered if either of you imagined what might have happened."

The silence told him that this was his cliff edge that he had to face alone.

He plunged on: "How did it feel? The two of them held onto each other, dropping down the cliff face. The rocks seemed so dangerous and huge. But they could sense that the sea was even bigger – stretching away to the far horizon. Sandy knew that the water was deep beneath the cliff. She often swam here. But Sam was not a good swimmer. If they managed to reach the water, she would have to make sure that Sam was safe and help him to the shore. All these thoughts flashed through her mind in a split second. Meanwhile Sam imagined how angry Gregory would be if they managed to escape, yet again. And if they made it back to land, he knew Gregory would not give up the chase.

The immense splash as they hit the water sent spray high up the cliff face. As the water sprinkled down, Gregory's men could make out the tiny figures in the water far below. Sandy was swimming with one arm around Sam, ensuring that he could stay afloat as they slowly made their way to the beach.

"Get back down there and catch them!" Gregory shouted. But he knew that by the time his men had run down the long cliff path, Sam and Sandy would have long gone. And, indeed, ignoring their wet clothes, the two of them caught the coastline bus. Gregory's men found no sign of either of them. But they knew the bus service's terminus was at Northend and guessed that that is where the two were heading. So, driving in a small convoy of vehicles with Gregory at the front, they set off towards Northend. But Sam and Sandy had jumped off the bus long before Northend so were able to continue their mission. Would they be able to complete it successfully? Would they manage to get some dry clothes? No one can know the answer until the next instalment of this exciting story, tomorrow night."

Graham bent over to kiss his twins good night: but they had both dozed off the moment they knew Sam and Sandy were safe.

# SCALPEL

I was not looking forward to the operation. I knew all patients had a right to be fearful. The pre-op procedure had been taken by a young nurse – she could have been a schoolgirl. I was not confident she knew what she was doing. I could imagine the headline after a botched job in the operating theatre following fatal short cuts at the pre-op stage: "Impatience kills patient: hospital apologises."

I spent so much time here that I already felt I knew about the lives of most of the staff. And despite, or maybe because of, their fulsome encouragement, I felt a deep sense of trepidation. I knew that this was an extremely unusual operation; and it would normally be carried out by an eminent surgeon. I did not find it any more reassuring to be told that there would be video recordings made of the procedure for use in medical school training programs.

The day of the operation was bright and clear. That morning, my wife said, "Don't be afraid, you're about to become a celebrity!" The staff were quietly cheerful and pleasantly professional. I sensed that they were all trying to make me feel calm and confident. The theatre had to be one-hundred-percent sterile: you could smell and taste the disinfectant.

White-coated viewers were already perched above in the observation lounge. The anaesthetist was busy with equipment. The nurses' faces were all covered with surgical masks. The next five hours were going to be critical.

I reached out my hand and called 'Scalpel'.

# TALE OF A BYGONE AGE

## DAY 1

I do not expect popularity. The role of School Inspector is necessarily intrusive. My official visit to this local primary school was memorable.

It is difficult to forget stories narrated by an impressive speaker. As a child, that could be your mother. But as an adult, it is rare to find a reader who can make such impact. You have left behind childish imaginings. You cannot be taken in by the cheap fairy tale tricks of malevolent monsters, terrifying tyrants, fickle fairies, saintly sages, passionate princes and beautiful brides.

So, it was a smile of recognition when I overheard the teacher say to her little pupils: "Now, children, I want you all to sit quietly and I'll tell you a story."

This was the most effective way of quietening the noisy youngsters after they had been running around wildly in the playground. As an official, I stopped to hear if her ploy proved to be effective. Also, I could not help noticing the unassuming beauty of the speaker.

"I want you to raise your hand if you have ever heard of how the daughter of an ancient king travelled across the seas in search of her grandfather's magic ring that she was told had been hidden on an island."

None of the youngsters moved.

"Well, I can tell you what happened. But you will have to sit very still because I must concentrate to remember it all.

"

It is a very exciting story, and I would not want to miss anything out by being disturbed. So, do any of you need the toilet before I begin?"

There was a wave of shaking heads: she knew very well that they had all just been. But she wanted to ensure that they concentrate on the story – a good trick when narrating to kids.

"Diana was the king's daughter. She kissed her daddy goodbye and set off on her boat, loaded with food and drink.  She had insisted on bringing her pet frog, Rana and, after a week, they arrived at the first island. Rana warned Diana not to go ashore. "This island is where giant snakes live. It is rumoured that they even swallow elephants! The snakes only fear the enormous birds, the rocs, whose massive talons can snatch up a snake before flying it back to their nest for a family feast. The island is magic, and its valleys are carpeted with diamonds. One legend speaks of brave men outrunning the snakes and tossing huge chunks of meat into the valley. The birds carry the meat back to their nests, then the men collect the diamonds stuck to the meat when the rocs leave the nest in search of another meal."

But Diana did not believe a word of it. "That's just a fairy tale," she said as she boldly set off in search of the ring. It was not long before she heard the snap of twigs and rustling of leaves in the undergrowth. She stopped and watched to see what was making the sound. Two green eyes suddenly appeared over the bush. Diana took a step back, but it was too late to avoid the touch on her back made by the tongue of another huge serpent. She spun around just as the snakes from behind the bush slithered forward: and one bit her leg. She screamed with pain and fainted. The snakes moved away to let the giant queen serpent come and inspect who they had trapped. But before the queen serpent could arrive, Rana had heard Diana's scream and came leaping to her. He picked her up onto his back and froggy jumped as fast as he could back to the ship. The queen serpent was furious and, together with her army of poisonous snakes, came wriggling after them. As the ship moved away from the shore, the sailors breathed a sigh of relief. But if they thought that the sea would frighten the queen snake, they were sadly mistaken. She launched herself into the water and started swimming quickly towards them. The serpent was swimming faster than them! How could they escape? Suddenly a great shadow fell across the bow of the ship. The biggest bird ever seen came swooping down. The king of the rocs seized the queen snake and flew off.

Rana rubbed some magic ointment on where the snake had bitten Diana. The poison leaked out and she recovered. "Thank you for saving me," she said. "But I still need to find the magic ring. Perhaps we might have more luck on the next island." When they arrived, it did not feel like the island of the snakes. Instead, it was covered with lovely fruit trees and beautiful flowers. In the centre of the island, a mountain rose up to the clouds. Perhaps the ring might be high up in one of the mountain caves, taken there by inquisitive magpies that like to collect shiny objects. So, Diana and Rana climbed slowly up the mountain until they came to the highest cave. Afraid that a monster would leap out of the darkness, Diana drew her sword. But a different sort of magic suddenly pulled the sword from her hands and dumped it against a rock at the cave entrance. Diana had never come across a magnet before, but this is when she discovered how iron and steel can be pulled out of your hands if you stand beside a strong magnet. She prised the sword free and with Rana walked quickly back down the mountain, carrying a lump of the magnetic rock. She told the crew all about the stone that had seized her sword.

Perhaps it might be useful when they reach the next island."

The pretty teacher smiled and took a deep breath. "Now if you all behave, I'll tell you what happened when Diana and Rana reached the crystal island, and the island where fruits laugh and cry, and the island whose people live underwater, and the island with the magic horse. Also, I could tell you about the great desert they had to cross, the battleground they witnessed and the robot island whose brass horseman alone knew where the magic ring was hidden. Would you like to hear about that tomorrow?"

"Yes please," I shout and blush as the kids look round at me.

DAY 2.

Having embarrassed myself with my enthusiastic response to the teacher's question the day before, I decided I would sit quietly at the back of the classroom and try not to say anything whilst she addressed the children today.

I felt too shy to ask the beautiful teacher her name. But by inspecting the school's teaching rota, I had discovered she was also called Diana. I could imagine myself asking for her phone number, address and whether she would like to have dinner with me. But, as I was in the school on strictly official business, this would have been a gross breach of professional conduct. But I still experienced an involuntary, sharp intake of breath as Diana entered the room. She wore that carefree beauty of a young woman unaware of just how attractive her graceful movements and intimately warm speech were.

"I hope you don't mind, but I thought I would like to hear just how you are going to continue your story from yesterday."

Diana smiled, nodded, and said, "Of course, you are

only doing your job.”

The sinking feeling in my stomach told me that she saw me as the mere reporter of teaching technique. To her, I was not the man she was likely to agree to sharing a dinner after hours. The children filed in, ready for their lesson. But what can you teach a five-year-old in a class of thirty? Your best hope of influencing their educational future was to engross them in stories before you ever introduce them to published texts. And, after the previous day’s performance, I could already see how Diana was the perfect purveyor of scintillating tales.

“Do you remember what happened when Diana and Rana went to sea? Why were they in the boat sailing across the seas?”

One tiny tot put up her hand and said, “Diana wants to find the magic ring, miss.”

“That’s right. But did they find it on the first island?”

All the children spoke in one voice, “No!”

The same child added, “They just escaped the snakes.”

“And what about the second island?” Diana asked.

“They found the magnetic rock,” another child piped up.

“That’s right. But they took the magnetic rock with them as they sailed toward the third island. On landing, Diana and Rana were amazed by the pretty colours that glittered in the stones by the shore. Diana wondered if one of the sparkling stones could have been the missing ring. Rana suggested that they could use the magnetic rock to try to disentangle the ring, if it was there, from all the other glittering stones. So, they walked up and down the beach, holding the magnet before them in the hope of seeing the ring spring up. But, after an hour, the magnet had gathered nothing metallic, and Diana was feeling unhappy. “Will I ever find my grandfather’s magic ring?” she asked. Rana reassured her. "Just because all these glistening crystals do not include the ring does not mean that they are any less beautiful. When we find beauty, we should enjoy it for itself, Diana."

I looked at Diana and was unsure whether she glanced at me with these last words. Perhaps I was imagining it.

"The fourth island was magic. Diana had left the magnet on the ship and gone ashore alone. Rana had stayed behind to oversee repairs that were needed on the boat. But Diana was not afraid. She was just astonished at the trees loaded with fruit. She felt tempted to pick an apple from one of the low-hanging branches. Imagine her surprise when the apple spoke! "Hello. Are you hungry? Please feel free to pick me off this tree." Suddenly Diana heard a huge chorus of other apples shouting, "Yes, Diana. Pick the apple or he will just go mouldy." She plucked the apple and decided that it would be selfish if she returned to the ship as the only one with any fruit to eat. So, she gathered an armful of ripe apples, ready to hand them round to the whole crew. The tree from where she had picked the fruit seemed full of laughter as the fruit celebrated her selection. But as she passed by another tree, the sound of weeping disturbed her. "Why are you crying? she asked. "None of us were fortunate enough to find you nearby when we were ripe," a plump pear said. "But now we are all so over-ripe that we are all destined to just drop off the tree and lie, rotting, until the next year's crop."

The school bell rang. Today was a short lesson. Diana stood up. "Now I want you all to walk quietly to the hall for the music and dance period. Tomorrow, if you like, I can finish the story of Diana and Rana. Would you like that?"

The children, remembering my outburst from the day before, all turned towards me! I stood up and faced Diana. "What stories will you tell us tomorrow?"

She replied, and the children looked up at us, overhearing our conversation. "Well, there are people who live underwater all their lives. Diana and Rana will learn many things from them. Then, they might try to ride a magic horse across the vast desert where terrible battles were fought. Then, hopefully, they will find the brass horseman on the robot island who, alone, knows where to find the magic ring."

As the children filed out, I said, "I am looking forward to that."

DAY 3.

The final day of the school inspection arrived. I had already written my report and would deliver it to the head teacher and the Government Inspection Department at the end of the day. Meanwhile, all I could really think about was the lovely teacher.

Her story continued and I was enraptured by the way it was delivered.

"The submarine civilisation was unknown to Diana, although Rana had heard about it from frog gossip. Granted the magical power to breathe underwater, Diana and Rana dived down and swam freely amongst the buildings and highways that had been constructed by the inhabitants of the deep seas. Here they found that disagreements were resolved without fighting. They had no swords like Diana's. Instead, they could appeal to the ultimate judges whose decisions were never questioned. Indeed, to have tried to fight against the presiding whales and the sharks who enforced the laws would have been pointless, even dangerous. So, Diana and Rana discovered a wonderfully peaceful place that contrasted sharply with what awaited them next."

"The final island was huge. To get across to the other side, they thought they would need a camel as a sandy desert stretched out as far as they could see. Diana told her sailors to stay safe on the ship as she and Rana started to walk over the first dusty dune. Imagine their surprise when, once the crew were out of sight, they came across a funny-looking donkey. "The donkey spoke to the frog. "Are you Rana?" Rana nodded. "Good. I have a job to do. Will you and your mistress mount onto my back please." Diana was not sure if the old donkey could carry their weight. But Rana hopped on and sat there awaiting Diana. The moment she settled into the saddle, the donkey transformed into a huge horse with fine, white wings. "Are you both ready?" the magic horse asked. Rana called "Yes", and the horse began to trot. After a couple of minutes and he could sense that Diana and Rana were comfortable, he began to canter. The sand started to fly up behind them. After a few more minutes, with a great NEIGH, the gallop was launched, and it felt as if they had taken off. They were moving so fast that both Diana and Rana had to hold onto the saddle tightly so as not to be blown off.

After an hour, they suddenly arrived at the desert's end. Here was a stretch of land strewn with the bodies of hundreds of soldiers where war had finally fizzled out when there were no more young men left to fight. Instead, both sides had constructed a huge robot. They stood facing one another, each knowing that whoever moved first would be destroyed. "Where can we go from here?" Rana whispered to Diana. "Look!" Diana pointed to the streaking rush of another horse carrying the imposing figure of an upright rider made entirely from brass. The brass horseman dismounted and wobbled unsteadily over to Diana and Rana who, obediently, dismounted from their steed. Slowly, the horseman opened his hand and there, twinkling in the dying light, was her grandfather's magic ring. Diana smiled with delight as Rana took the ring and placed it on her finger. She put her arms around her faithful frog and kissed him on his lips. With a flash of recognition, she found she was embracing the most handsome prince of her imagination."

I picked up an elastic band that was lying on the children's desk and tentatively placed it on Diana's fourth finger. But before we could kiss, the children burst into the classroom to hear the end of the story.

# PASSING THROUGH

Passing through on his horse, Lord Arbuthnot Manners banged his head on oak's overhanging branch. Hundreds of people had passed through this glade and never once had anyone knocked into the trunk or branches, nor even slipped on the carpet of Autumn leaves oak laid down. But Manners was livid as if oak had deliberately cudgelled him to the ground. As he limped away, he swore he would have oak's branch removed.

After the sun rose the next day, oak was visited by a couple of youngsters. Neither wanted to cut the tree but Manners had given orders, and they would not be paid until they presented him with the severed branch. One rested a rickety ladder against oak's trunk. He held it steady as his mate climbed carefully. The ladder did not feel secure as oak's bark was slippery after overnight rain. But, as the morning progressed, the saw used by the climber gradually cut a deep groove into the branch. He could have snapped the branch off by pushing down on the branch once it had been cut half through. But he knew that this would leave the beautiful tree looking ugly. When they had finished their work, they carefully stripped the dead branch of its twigs and leaves as the old oak swayed and creaked above them. Then one balanced the ladder on his shoulder whilst the other carried the branch back to Manners to claim the reward.

Regrowing the branch took many sunrises. Over those years, oak's trunk slowly grew fatter. A young couple – no relation to the Manners family – were courting when Jay, the husband-to-be, took it into his head to use a pen knife to carve his loved-one's initials on oak's bark. Unfortunately, her name was Linda Ann Meadow. Oak wondered whether the LAM initials were an inadvertent memorial to the clumsy Lord's accident.

Winters found the snow pressing heavily on the branches of neighbouring trees. Occasionally, they snapped. But Oak was far sturdier than the surrounding youngsters. With Spring, most melting lumps slithered down the trunk. But the newly grown overhang had its own notions about how to deposit its load. Oak worried that this could lead to a reprise of the Manners performance of two centuries ago if the cascade hit a passing traveller. The child of Jay and Linda stood beneath the branch and opened her arms, laughing, as the flakes showered down on her. There would be no Manners anger here.

Oak was patient with the slowly evolving landscape. The nearby river flooded more often and some of the water even reached the base of oak's trunk. The birds flitting through oak's leaves had been almost exclusively sparrows and blackbirds in Manners's day. Now oak found aggressive crows and magpies sparring for space. The spiders and tiny insects were still in residence right through from Spring until the end of Autumn, yet the birds seemed to fly away before the annual larvae emerged. Despite producing large quantities of acorns, oak knew that almost all would be eaten up by squirrels and birds … but oak did not really mind. They were just staying alive: the opposite to men like Manners who were inclined towards random acts of violent destruction.

It was Autumn and LAM had faded away many decades ago. Walking through the glade that presented a glorious Klimt-like image of red and gold, I acknowledged the fine oak with its overhanging branch. And oak could see that I was no engraver or cutter. I was just passing through.

# LONG LIFE

We were relieved that someone was finally doing something about overcrowding. Being told that there was plenty of room for people to live here did not correspond with our everyday experience.

"There are vast uninhabited areas. We can build new accommodation and spread the population more evenly across the land," my wife claimed.

"You can say that but, in reality, no one would be able to survive out there. There are no facilities, no services, no schools, no jobs. People need to live in the cities unless you are a landowner growing crops," I replied.

"We could change all that. We could build new towns with all the needs of the population met without the hopeless mess we've created in the cities."

"In theory you are right. But the last time this was seriously proposed, you know what happened. No one was willing to divert resources into such an enormous program with no guarantee of success. So, finally, we have this new policy for which people voted."

I knew more about this as I had been involved with the development of the anti-ageing drug, Bùlǎo, (不老 in Chinese) whose success had multiplied the overcrowding problems. My own grandfather had recently celebrated his hundred and fiftieth birthday and our house/hotel with its numerous extensions and additional floors was bulging with five of his children, fifteen of his grandchildren, and fifty-nine of his great grandchildren.

My wife commented on how well and handsome I looked at one hundred and twenty. I refrained from saying anything about her appearance for any comment would be instantly interpreted as either directly insulting or ridiculously untrue. As the elected representative of our region, I was accustomed to making politically tactful comments. And officially, I met representatives from other nations who reported similar issues amongst their people.

It seemed inevitable that their leaders and ours would come to an international solution to this shared problem. As geriatrics across the globe had become irrevocably attached to Bùlǎo, the solution could not be found with the traditional processes of passing away with age. So, the carefully staged conflict during which most under-fifties perished finally gave us the breathing room our leaders had promised.

# ACHILLES

I was not stupid. I knew that Hector felt he had been snubbed when I was appointed in charge of Planet Transport. He had been the deputy, but Command had decided to transfer me from Head of Robotics for reasons that still escape me. Colleagues say they understand why. I am assured that Hector has always been a harsh boss whereas I try to incentivise young recruits to learn lessons in a spirit of mutual support.

The trade in Zoí probably sours most relations, so I cannot entirely blame Hector for his permanently dour mood. Its rarity encourages thieves to invade the grimy, Greek storage chambers. Occasionally, Command permits this thieving of Zoí to succeed, and the gang's triumphant trumpeting of their success ensures that there are always plenty of others who try to imitate their exploits. But the chambers are a honey trap. Once inside, the robbers are within the Planet Transport field that whisks them through the space-time gate and lands them, unceremoniously, at the feet of the Achilles robots that patrol the hot, red planet, Zoí. In effect, Command has made Zoí into a secretive penal colony where thieves are forced to dig for what they had wanted to steal.

I had been replacing a Picard Tube that had been damaged within the chamber. Hector was outside to ensure that the chamber was decommissioned whilst I was at work. The moment I plugged in the Picard, he switched on the Transport Field. Dangerous and criminal! It is a miracle that without proper forcefield strapping I was not spread like an infinite pack of cards across the space-time continuum between home and Zoí. Instead, I was deposited face down in the iron-rich mud beside the Zoí mine complex.

The gleaming Model A Achilles robot that stood over me commanded that I stand. I knew everything that anyone knew about the Model A as I had created the first ones as Head of Robotics. I knew that it was useless to resist an Achilles: even the Model A had stronger limbs than a three-ton pumping iron. But I also knew exactly where the power switch was located as I had flicked the Model A on and off hundreds of times. I could navigate the cleverly disguised switch in my sleep. So, I said "Yes, sir," to the robot as if I was about to obey the order to pull myself up. But at the same time, I reached out to the left heel and carried out the circular motion that cut the power. I switched him off.

When I stood up, I could see other Model A robots corralling unwilling colonists to work. No doubt they would be returned, dusty and exhausted, to their sleeping quarters at the end of the day. The intention of the inventors of this piece of cruelty was to sicken the thieves with the sight and feel of Zoí. Months and months of handling Zoí also destroys the tissue around their fingers and wrists. I knew that everyone dies on Zoí eventually as no one has ever been transported back. I was determined to break this dismal tradition.

Reprogramming the guard robot that had been sent to bring me in was not easy. It was years since I had worked on an Achilles. Nowadays, I knew that most programming on Model A robots was carried out by flame-retardant, supposedly hyper-intelligent, Model Bs. There was no way that I could emulate the sophistication and speed of their work. But I remembered enough to have this robot obey my voice commands.

"Take me to the Communications Tower." And the robot seized me by the shoulder and led me uncomplaining past the other robot guards who sensed that I was being delivered somewhere especially unpleasant by Command. Once inside the impersonal Tower block, my robot deposited me at the grey Comms unit where daily reports were created and sent back home. It took me less than a minute to report that an unknown man had failed to arrive and was almost certainly spread thinly across space-time without any chance of restitution. I requested advice as to how to proceed and imagined Hector happily responding that nothing could or should be done.

I called my robot Data 1. The question for me was how to approach Data 2, 3, 4, 5 etcetera. And if I did manage to control the Achilles robots on Zoí, what was I to do with the men and women I would be releasing from the mines? I had to remember that some of them were vicious thugs whose departure from the home planet had been celebrated by their victims. Perhaps I should program Data 1 to be my personal protection guard.

Despite continuing to deluge home with reassuring messages reporting all was well on Zoí, it was becoming clear to Command that something must be wrong. The supply of the valuable mineral started drying up with convicts being released as I reprogrammed their guards one by one. I spoke with bedraggled prisoners who did not seem to be hardened criminals. Most just seemed relieved to be freed from the violent authority exercised by the robots. Tired and dishevelled, they were looking to me to decide how we could escape the planet.

I knew that everything would change if Model Bs arrived. I had no way of knowing how to reprogram this later model that had been developed after I had left Robotics. If I was going to act decisively, it would have to be soon. Queries being sent to us at the Comms Tower implied that Command was clearing the way for a Model B team to arrive once they could be brought together at the storage chambers.

Fortunately, I discovered Scotty amongst the prisoners, and I knew his reputation as an engineer. Apparently, he had been transported due to a ridiculous accident where the induction field was affected by a temporary energy burst. This pulled him into the chamber's field although, at the time, he was innocently walking past on his way home. We had studied at university together and he was as amazed as I was when we saw each other outside the mine entrance.

Without interference from the robots, Scotty was able to invert the Transport Field generator. He and I selected half a dozen reliable Model As to accompany us into the Comms Tower where the Model Bs were due to be transported the next day. It was a tense few hours before the Transport link was activated and I half expected that both of us would disintegrate with our accompanying robots. No one had ever attempted to construct an inverse field which would fling us to the spot from where the Model Bs had departed.

There was a flash. Scotty and I instinctively seized each other's hands. Then we both breathed a huge sigh of relief on arriving intact, unsteady but upright! We smiled at one another and looked around. At that very moment I spotted Hector skulking around. Data 1 seized him and threw him to the ground before Scotty and me.

"I thought you were dead!" he shouted when he saw me standing over him.

"You nearly killed me." I told him. "Command should have you prosecuted for attempted murder."

Hector was beside himself and furious at seeing me there, very much alive. He leapt up and lunged towards me, but he never made it. My Achilles robot lanced him in the neck with one of its spear attachments. The man convulsed and opened his mouth to speak but the spear had severed his vocal cords, so there were no last words to be heard.

Scotty ran to the Comms link to discover what was happening on Zoí. Apparently, the Model B team of six robots was overwhelmed by the sixty Model As that I had reprogrammed. My message to Command explained what had happened and I asked to resume my post in charge of Planet Transport. The lack of response annoyed Scotty. He declared we should physically climb up the steps to Command to speak to those in charge face to face.

We walked in unchallenged. "Good morning, Transport Director Paris," I was being addressed directly by the sole occupant of the Command post. "I do not care how you acquire it, but I cannot survive without a regular supply of Zoí," boomed the Master Model C.

# SWEETNESS AND LIGHT

She had that glow which cannot be cosmetically manufactured. I had no idea of her age, but she spoke about her grandchildren with affection. As her descriptions illuminated a happy childhood and her voice lilted with a smiling recollection of years spent abroad, I realised that her knowledge of world events and other lands far outstripped my ignorant and superficial understanding. But she was not arrogant: I never felt that she was talking down to me. She just enjoyed thinking back to pleasant years working with her husband, bringing up her kids and joining in neighbourhood fun and games.

Her breadth of reading was impressive. I believed that my semi-distinguished career lecturing on aspects of English literature would provide me with a range of recommendations to swap with her. But almost every work I spoke about she had not only read but, far more impressively, could recall in sufficient detail to provide an informed critique. There were moments when I thought she could have undertaken my old job.

Her home was tastefully decorated with only a tiny selection of *objets d'art*. But every item had a history that she would recount with relish. These were never intended as a means by which to show off. Instead, each disclosed aspects of her own interests, past occupations and insights into people and places that were important to her.

It had been many years since her husband had passed away. She recounted the pain of his final months before cancer took him. She spoke with pride how her children had gathered to support her and their unswerving commitment ensuring she would never feel left out, abandoned and alone. I smiled with regret at the contrast with how my daughter and son treated me. I did not mention this: I did not want sympathy. Instead, I liked hearing how her family could stand as a model to which we might all aspire.

I was curious when she said her husband had been an inventor whose creativity had brought the family significant wealth. I remembered her telling me that one of her sons was a pilot, selected for training as an astronaut. "Was this the area where your husband had contributed?" Apparently not. Then I noticed a framed photograph of a girl whom I correctly guessed was of her daughter joining the navy as a senior officer – a major achievement for any woman! But although pride at her daughter's racing up the ranks was well deserved, it had no relevance to her husband's innovation.

After a wonderful meal that she had cooked for us, she sat down and performed on the grand piano that dominated the drawing room at the back of her house. Her impeccable musicianship would have impressed a legion of classical music critics. Instead, she just enjoyed creating this intimate sound purely for our private pleasure. Eventually, I could not contain my curiosity any longer to discover what invention had made the family so comfortable and permitted our charming hostess an ideal retirement.

She pointed to a standard pill box with the words 'sweetness and light' printed across the side. "These medically approved, mass-produced pills provide an ecstatic experience which takers describe as "sweetness and light" seconds before they expire."

# EULOGY

There is no one in this congregation who does not have a tale to tell about Vincent. Standing over a foot above most of us, he would look down with his imposing presence and speak with that rumbling bass voice. And what did he say?

I am sure that he knew more prayers and invocations than most of our full-time priests. If ever there was a man closer to Heaven, both spiritually and physically, I have yet to meet him.

Most of us will remember his kindness, his gentle treatment of those whom he met, and the love he showed to all his wives and most of his children. But, above all, he was a Christian Soldier who always knew he was marching to war every day. Woe betide anyone who crossed him on his path of righteousness!

Some of you may recall the terrible times when the two crime families in our region were rampant. Only Vincent could have brought them to heel in his unique way.

"You need con-Vincing!" he told Paddy, the head of the most violent family. "I am imposing a *non jurandum* on your family."

Paddy laughed and said, "What the fuck is a *non jurandum?*" Vince explained that it was a ban on swearing which would be punished each time the ban was broken. "You have broken it just now, Paddy, so I am fining you a hundred dollars which will go to the Church widows and orphans fund."

"I'm not bloody well paying," Paddy was stupid enough

to respond.

"Ah well," Vincent replied. "I will explain to everyone in the Parish that you despise the widows and orphans – unlike Gerry, who has already paid up when a bad word slipped out."

We all know limping Gerry who lost his left foot when one of his improvised explosive devices accidentally detonated – or so we are told. Of course, Paddy did not want the shame of being compared in such a bad light to the head of the other crime family. So, he paid up. Then Vincent played the same trick on Gerry.

When he taught the kids at the Sunday school, the priests were delighted as he seemed to hit it off with youngsters in a way almost impossible for any man of the cloth. The children of Paddy's and Gerry's family, regular attenders of Vincent's classes, never swore. It was the beginning of peace in our neighbourhood.

It was his piety that brought about his demise. It was the sight of Gerry and Paddy shaking hands and embracing that made him exclaim "Well, Lord, strike me dead!"

# FLIGHT TIMES

Fred had always been a gambling man. If there were no races taking place, he would find something else upon which to bet. He was obviously addicted, losing money regularly. Fortunately, with no wife or children at home and his parents having died many years ago, he had no dependents to suffer from his addiction. Without the regular income from his clerical job, he would have been seen merely as just another unsuccessful, semi-professional gambler. But he liked to think of himself as an expert on horse racing, keeping a statistical account of how the odds on individual horses altered with the weather, the race conditions and their standings according to the most popular race commentators.

He was over fifty before he began to have suspicions about the way that the gambling industry operated. He was not stupid and knew that, in the final analysis, the only winners were the bookmakers. If they were long-term losers, there would be no gambling industry. But he was such an inveterate gambler, an almost permanent fixture in the High Street bookies, that the record he kept of his bets created a massive and impressive database. It was only after he cross-referenced this record against his statistical account that he believed he had discovered a pattern, completely hidden from the average punter.

Fred decided to apply this hard-won knowledge to his betting. Soon he found himself netting a noticeable income from the local bookie. Online winnings were even more impressive, which was just as well after he was banned when the locals found themselves losing money to him. He began enjoying a unique experience, earning money from gambling! "You have the most diabolical luck," Jake told him. Jake was Fred's only friend – another permanent fixture at the High Street bookmaker who refused to go back there once they banned Fred. Fred said nothing to Jake about the system he had carefully developed.

Jake was heartbroken when he witnessed the accident. The car, driven by an eighty-year-old who should not have been behind the wheel of any vehicle, clipped the kerb where Fred was walking. The car swerved out of control and flipped across the pavement, crushing Fred. Jake ran across the road to help his friend, but Fred was already dead. The driver was arrested, his driving license confiscated and sentenced to community service that he was physically incapable of carrying out. Fred's meagre winnings were left to Jake, and his system went with him. Throughout his life Fred had committed very few sins; he led a boringly unblemished life. He soon found heavenly existence offered little chance of bringing his system into operation on this higher plain.

Jake would have been proud of his mate's capacity for discovering betting possibilities, even when they were expressly forbidden by the Authorities. He had been chatting with a couple of saintly do-gooders when he noticed that each time one of them started showing off one of his earthly accomplishments, a minuscule angel (an anglette) would flit down, land on the boaster's shoulder and whisper a warning against pride in the ear of the minor miscreant.

He met two old Greek philosophers clearly bored with their Elysian existence. They told him that every innovation and discovery made here was already known by the

Authority, every branch of mathematics and metaphysics already totally covered. He asked what they thought brought forth the anglette: was it simply boasts? Perhaps more egregious boasts would bring forth faster anglette intervention? Being curious about their surroundings (however tedious) was one of the key characteristics of geniuses. So, Aristotle said, "we should set up an experiment."

His companion was unsure whether any experiment could ever reveal the truth behind any observation. But as Plato had nothing else to do, he agreed to participate.

Fred said he would act as the clock (there were no timepieces here as he had been assured that time did not "really" exist – whatever that meant). But Aristotle said out loud, emphasising every word just to ensure that an anglette would know how bad his admission was.

"I two-timed my lover and never told him about it." An anglette floated down and spoke reassuringly into his ear.

Plato took his turn. "I planned to murder my lover when I found he had been two-timing me."

Another anglette streaked down and shouted a reprimand in Plato's ear.

Fred said: "Aristotle's took ten seconds: Plato's took two!"

Chatting to others and challenging them to predict how long it would take to attract an anglette brought forward a wide variety of guesstimates.

"We won't use money," he suggested. "After all, there is no use for cash here. We'll just play this game for fun." With this suggestion he hoped to escape any Authority restrictions on what he assumed would be regarded as a vice. And sure enough, the first round when he whispered a continuously recurring lewd thought brought a five second anglette. He congratulated the bemused winner, a girl who had died aged three so never had much opportunity to become a sinner (apart from a tiny drop of the original variety) and had only learnt to count to five.

Where most small-time gamblers would have been satisfied with carving out this tiny, hallowed corner where inconspicuous odds could be laid, Fred started to set his sights on something more ambitious. The next time he managed to attract an anglette onto his shoulder, he swung around suddenly and seized the unsuspecting little one. "What do you want?" the anglette demanded, struggling to break free. "I just want to ask you something. I promise not to hurt you."

After hearing Fred's proposal, the anglette nodded and flew off. As time did not exist here, Fred instantly found himself acting as a unique celestial bookie, taking bets from all and sundry guessing on the timing of friendly anglette flights. But instead of earning vast sums of earthly wealth to spend on whatever he desired; Fred was awarded a free holiday to a resort with an unbelievably hot climate.

# CHEVAUCHÉE

"Listen, my son," the General, was speaking. I attended closely because he became angry if I failed to take in all he said. At the Military Academy, he was known for his short temper. As a father he was always attentive to my needs as a child. But now, having reached the mature age of thirteen, he regarded me as an adult. He was away shouting orders at the Academy recruits on parade when my mother asked me what I wanted to do when I grew up. I whispered I would like to learn to play the piano and become a musician. She advised me strongly to keep this ambition to myself. "Your father might not like to hear that."

The General came home and took me aside. I was embarrassed because I was anticipating an awful session where he thought he was doing every father's duty – to explain the reproductive process and the necessity of using contraceptives during sexual intercourse. I dreaded this as he would undoubtedly stray into declaring homosexuality a perversion that he would not tolerate in any child of his. At thirteen, I had little idea about my sexuality as I had not had any opportunity to try it out. Although I was probably not a homosexual, I could see no reason to regard any friend who thought he was as less of a friend.

"Now listen, my son," I was already groaning inwardly. "There are certain things that every young man needs to know. It took me some years to realise how important what I am about to divulge to you will be for your life. Although you will have many years before you to practise what is, at your age, just theory. It is never too early to be introduced to these critical facts of life.”

I was starting to get bored; but had to restrain myself. Implying how ridiculous this speech was would have been seen as a gross display of indiscipline. But he was pausing and looking to me, as if awaiting some show of attendance.

“Yes, sir.” I nodded as if encouraging him to carry on.

“Very well,” he continued as he turned to his desk. I started to shiver with horror. ‘Oh my God!’ I thought to myself. ‘I do hope he is not about to open his drawer and reveal a display of condoms and other apparatus associated with sex.’ I was starting to sweat and blush. I took out my handkerchief as if to blow my nose: it was just an excuse to cover my mouth and face to hide whatever involuntary expressions he might cause.

“Right. I want no excuses. There is nothing more important than Sun Tzu’s ‘The Art of War’ and Machiavelli’s ‘The Prince’. They are essential reading.” And he placed the books on the desk for me to take. I took a sharp intake of breath: I have no idea if this was shock or relief. But he took it to be a good sign.

“I am glad to see how excited you feel about being introduced to these two masters. As a young man, you will find them essential reading in everything you do and, especially, when you are older and take command of troops.”

I decided there and then to go along with the General’s wish. After all, what harm could there be in reading a couple of books? Mother was clearly unimpressed: I think she was hoping that I would improve myself by reading classic literature. But, for the sake of peace with the General, I read both Machiavelli’s and Sun Tzu’s famous works. He told mother he was delighted to find me reading Sun Tzu – an author whom he regarded as superior to such a poor player as William Shakespeare or a weak peacenik like Leo Tolstoy. Then, to cap it all, he was appointed as Director of the Military Academy! My ambition to become a professional musician looked more distant than ever as we went to live in the grounds of the Academy – surrounded by recruits more intent upon keeping khaki clean than pursuing pianistic perfection.

Mother knew I was unhappy but felt unable to support my ambition. For her, being the Academy Director's wife gave her all the status she craved. How her son coped with his musical dreams against the reality of family life was up to him to resolve. It is ironic how the solution to my dilemma was presented through a profound understanding of the teaching of my father's author heroes.

The one interest I shared with the Academy recruits was the latest electronic war games. The earliest had leaned heavily upon spectacular graphics and the challenge of speedy responses to 'enemy' appearances on screen. But with the dawn of the avatar-based games where the player imagined himself to be at one with his selected avatar on screen, a new fantasy life was being presented. The addictive qualities of the latest games were bound to affect students. Loss of attention to detail, a sharp decline in interest in their chosen area of study and the sheer amount of screen time craved and taken led to major problems for those in charge of educational institutions. It was me who deliberately introduced the latest game to the new recruits. Soon they all were playing the appropriately named Chevauchée. (A term commonly used in the 100 Years War but with startlingly new appeal to contemporary warmongers).

The General was defeated by one of the oldest strategies – the diversionary attack aimed at the demoralisation of his army. By the time he had learnt how to co-exist with an already defeated, distracted cohort of men, he had ceased attending to his wayward son. My career as a pianist began with a shelf containing all the Beethoven sonatas and Chopin studies alongside the texts of Machiavelli and Sun Tzu.

# SECOND SIGHT

After the intensive training, the astronauts now knew who would start on the historic journey. The seventy men and seventy women crew for each of the twelve craft understood this was a trip whose end they could never see. They would need to reproduce generations of pilots, engineers, doctors, and musician/artists during the voyage as the destination would not be reached for many centuries.

The greatest problems identified in early long-distance flights were psychological. The musician/artists were there to ensure that crew members engaged in thought-provoking and personally creative activities. That would only be for those who were not in suspended animation. Each member needed to experience deep sleep for a year every three years. This prolonged their own lifespans. And because tedious, unchanging patterns of behaviour had been identified as a major cause of aggravation and conflict, this ensured that the wake group was continuously altering, so enhancing interpersonal harmony.

Each of the Possel Craft had been constructed to house huge areas for arts and crafts, sport and exercise, entertainment, manufacturing, and luxurious living quarters. No expense had been spared in designing and constructing the dozen Possels that were parked orbiting the moon ready for their journey.

After the peaceful departure, the Possels maintained close contact with one another. But interchange of personnel between them was intermittent as it was believed that long-term relationships were best developed within the confines of each carefully constructed environment. Throwing out the balance between the internal groupings, let alone the potential disaster of creating inter-Possel amorous and sexual jealousies, required independence rather than interdependence between the twelve.

Noah Abraham, the captain of Peter (the lead Possel) was appointed for the initial flight out of the solar system. Ready for his first sleep suspension, he was happy to be handing over to Sarah East for the next phase because the journey out beyond the Kuiper Belt into the Oort Cloud held little interest. "When you've seen one icy rock you've seen them all," Sarah said to her musician/artists. "I think this is when your contribution to the crew's sanity will become critical." Her teenage son, Jacob, never looked out of the observation windows. For him, viewing passing dust was as boring as Sarah would have found studying static stratus cloud formations when she was a girl. Those born on board had little interest in what was outside their craft. For them, quite apart from personal relationships, their struggles were principally coping with the complexity of the compulsory engineering lectures whilst managing the excitement generated by the musicians' concerts.

Twelve months later Sarah East was sixty – quite old for suspended animation. Noah Abraham's time to reemerge from the suspension couch was due just before she was to take his place. Jacob suddenly showed interest in what this would involve. He was close to his mother and worried that he might not see her again. "When will you be reawakened?" he asked.

"I should be brought back next year. You remember Noah before he was suspended a year ago. You can ask him what it was like when you see him next week."

Noah, reawakened, was confused. The Equin-Amor

drug had different effects on sleepers. Most had no aftereffects but for some, like Noah, temporary disorientation after reawakening was common.

"Hello, who are you?" Noah asked as the room seemed to spin around a boy whom he thought he recognised.

"I'm Jacob. Please tell me what suspended animation felt like."

Noah had no instant recollection of what suspended animation was. For him, his last memory was falling asleep to music played by a quartet of musicians. He tried to grasp what felt just beyond his ability to recall and whispered: "Did you play in a string quartet?"

Jacob looked at Noah and wondered if the old man was losing his mind. Perhaps that was an effect of suspended animation. In which case, he did not want Sarah being put under. He grabbed hold of the sleep couch and started ripping out the control panel at the end of the bed. Noah watched him in a daze. Perhaps he was dreaming. To check if the young man was real, he reached out to touch his head. Jacob ducked out of the way, ran to the cabin door, and made his way as fast as he could to his mother.

"You mustn't get suspended!" he shouted to her. "It sends people crazy. I've just seen Noah and he is like a zombie. He tried to attack me." Sarah called her security patrol and marched up to where Noah should have been. But when they entered his cabin and found the sleep couch control panel in pieces, they decided that finding Noah was essential before he did any more damage.

Noah had wandered along the corridor from where he was sure he could smell food. "I'm ravishingly hungry," he announced as he sauntered into the dining area. The blazing eyes of a set of crew members he had never seen before stared at him. Noah was puzzled, wondering whether the Equin-Amor had any long-term aftereffects.

"Am I imagining you lot?" he asked as he staggered towards a tall stranger who seemed to hover. The apparition floated away from the tables, but Noah pursued him. "Don't run away, I want to talk to you." Another stranger with burning eyes intervened and held up his feathered hand to stop Noah. Noah was frustrated at being blocked. He was an accredited captain and had every right to question those on board. He shouted, "Get out of my way," and pushed towards the blocker. It was at that moment when Sarah and her security team walked into the dining hall.

Later, when he was resting in the medical chamber, Noah had recovered from what appeared to have been an electric shock. Sarah described to him the scene she and her team had witnessed.

"You were alone in the dining area and seemed to be having difficulty in getting past the tables. You shouted 'Get out of my way' although there was no one there. Then your hair stood on end, and you fell heavily, as if you had been electrocuted. We brought you here for treatment, but the doctor said you are perfectly fine now. We were concerned, especially after seeing how you had ripped up the control panel of your sleep couch."

Noah could not remember doing anything like that and Jacob was too embarrassed to admit to being the culprit.

"I think Equin-Amor may have affected my vision." Noah admitted. "Perhaps you could contact the other Possels to discover if those due to be awakened also saw what I saw. And he described the fiery-eyed men whom he had encountered – or imagined he had encountered.

Two of the other Possels reported similar incidents after crew awakenings.

"This cannot be simple hallucination," Noah said.

"Of course not," Sarah agreed. "Hallucinations do not deliver electric shocks."

Mark, the captain of Andrew Possel, had already held a staff conference after a senior female crew member had seen strangers who rose above her sleep couch. She insisted that the fire-eyed men in her bedroom were not familiar Andrew Possel members.

Lizzy, captain of Possel Simon, had to restrain a reawakened member who was thrashing about in a struggle with what she described as a Seraph whom no one else could see.

Mark and Lizzy had already decided that this must be a distressing side effect of Equin-Amor. But the electric shock delivered to Noah could not be explained as an Equin-Amor hallucination.

A rapidly convened conference of all twelve Possels was held on a craft where no one had shared this experience, just in case the hallucinations were connected in some way to the spatial location or indeterminate structural aspects of Simon, Andrew and Peter.

The John Possel had a pleasant, circular conference facility into which the forty men and women from all the Possels could be comfortably seated. Dick, the overweight captain of John, had collated all the reported information. He projected it onto the 3-d screens so that every representative was similarly appraised of what had occurred.

Tom, the captain of Possel Thomas, declared that he did not believe in the reality of what had been witnessed. "This must be an effect from the Equin-Amor, and perhaps the shock Noah experienced was a delayed build-up of charge from when he ripped out the control panel."

It was the team from Possel Judas who delivered the most alarming proposal. They reported that observations they had been making of the Oort cloud had been delivering remarkably repetitive results. Their chief science officer suggested that all the Possels should analyse the data he had collected to see if they would arrive at the same conclusion. "I think we might be in some sort of space-time loop. We appear to be progressing, but the data suggests that although moving forward, we seem to continually repeat identical observation results every couple of months. We twist and turn, but irrespective of how we position ourselves, the same observations return. We cannot escape it, it's as if we are caught within a Möbius Loop."

The Thomas team expressed doubts about Judas observations. Tom said: "If we believe everything we observe, then nothing makes sense as so much is self-contradictory. How can we be flying through the Oort cloud measurably distancing ourselves from the sun, yet caught in a loop which should fix us as stationary within a space-time bubble?"

It took the Bartholomew and Philip Possel teams to make the leap of faith that the others seemed unwilling to countenance. They had been in much closer contact with one another than any of the other Possels. Indeed, intermarriage between crew members that had been frowned upon from the outset, had been taking place, resulting in young offspring who took a much closer interest in what was happening outside the craft than children born on the other craft.

"We believe that these winged strangers are real. They must come from the destination to which we are all headed. They have been sent to help us out of the loop, or whatever you want to call the trough into which we have fallen, so that we can make our way forward again. But, because of time dilation, they do not appear before us as physical entities but, instead, projections who struggle to find a way to guide us. We think that Equin-Amor has an unanticipated side effect that produces a time-warped glimpse of our guides."

The Alpheusson, James, Thaddeus and Matthew teams remained perplexed at the confusing variety of theories. Matthew's musicians had even produced one of their own. Their leader, Marion, suggested that the twelve crafts were merely models held in a massive experimental chamber back on Earth. The strangers were just outside observers using full-colour wave band macro-scopes to review how all the crews were behaving in this vast intergenerational experiment. "The 'scopes feedback loops reflect floating images of the viewing researchers. The planets, the Kuiper Belt, the Oort cloud are being projected towards us as we imagine we are progressing through space-time. The observed repetitive loop shows the Research Team's lack of imagination. Unable to think how to project years and years of space travel's continuously changing environment, they just put us onto a repeating loop, so they didn't have to invent novel observations for us."

Noah listened to all these explanations of what he had experienced. Sarah asked him what he thought. "I'd like to know before I go into the sleep chamber," she said, "I'm quite anxious after what Jacob claims he saw when you emerged."

At that moment, Jacob walked into the room accompanied by an attractive girl whom neither Sarah nor Noah had met. "I think you should meet my girlfriend, Marion," he announced. "She is a fine musician, and we have been meeting on Matthew Possel."

Sarah frowned; "When have you been transporting across to Matthew?" she asked.

"Whenever you weren't looking," he replied.

Noah looked at Marion. "Are you the famous Maid Marion, the Matthew Musician all the Possels listen to?

"Yes, I'm Maid Marion." she replied, proudly.

Noah scrutinised her carefully. "But are you a really a

maid, Marion? Have you got something to tell us, young lady?"

Marion spoke directly to Noah. "You can see that I am pregnant, can't you?"

Noah nodded.

"So, you are going to be a father!" Sarah exclaimed, glaring at her son.

"I don't think so," Marion intervened. "We play music together…"

"…but we've never slept together," Jacob asserted.

"So, who is the father?" Sarah wanted to know.

"I am still a virgin. Unless someone drugged me with Equin-Amor, I am sure that Jacob nor anyone else has touched me."

"Are you telling us the truth, Jacob?" Noah demanded.

The young man took a deep breath and replied: "I've realised the truth is we are taking a message of beauty and wonder to the end of the Universe. But we, the carriers, will never know what it is."

There was a long silence as Jacob's words sank in. Noah struggled slowly to a seat. "Beauty and wonder!" He sensed this simple statement was, for him, a genuine epiphany.

Eventually Sarah asked, "How is your baby, Marion?"

"My doctor says he is strong and healthy. I imagine my son will be able to give us answers when he grows up, long after our generation has passed away."

"Perhaps you've been impregnated by one of these flying, fire-eyed strangers whilst you were asleep," Noah suggested.

"Stop teasing," Sarah told him.

"I doubt if we'll ever understand this mission," Noah said, "until we reach our destination and discover if anyone there can explain our journey better than all those we left behind."

# IMAGES

"The west front stained-glass windows are wonderful. The blue is so luminous when the sun is setting behind them. And the congregation marvels at the stories told by pictures. They seem to enjoy them like children love to hear a bedtime story from their mother. And whatever the story in the window depicts, it is treated as the truth – not like fairy stories told at bedtime."

"Yes, Rebecca, I understand."

"But, father, just think of the dedication and craft skills demonstrated by the glaziers. It must take years of training before they are able to create such masterpieces. I peeked inside one of the workshops last month and was alarmed by the sight of liquid lead being moulded by gloved hand, steam exploding from a sheet of glass being submerged in water and the scattered broken shards of glass lying across the floor. How can they focus on glass storytelling in such pandemonium?"

"They are an impressive set of craftsmen."

"I could not help noticing how the windows projected light that moved with the sun, making the images seem almost lifelike. By contrast, the gargoyles and statues feel gaunt and unmoving. Yet the masons chipping away at stone are just as dedicated. But I prefer the living quality of the warm glass."

"You are a sensitive viewer."

"Do we have any in our community to compare with these craft geniuses?"

Rebecca's father paused before replying. He wondered if this fascination for cathedral artistry would be the first step of his daughter being seduced into the Church. He worried that his wife would respond with fury, with hysteria, with incomprehension. But he also knew that Rebecca was speaking only to him. It was for him to respond, or she would undoubtedly share her perceptions with her mother!

"It has been difficult for our great artists to practise in this way, Rebecca, for we are not permitted to own land upon which we could establish monumental synagogues. And even if we could, you know we are specifically forbidden to create graven images. They become icons that detract from our rightful contemplation of the invisible presence of God. Instead, we are permitted to speak and write for in the beginning was the Word – so that is what we use to create masterpieces. You yourself have commented upon the beauty of expression when studying the Mishnah. And your admiration for Joseph is not purely enjoying the beauty of your future husband. His musical performances and lovely singing voice are, themselves, portable works of art."

Rebecca smiled. "Father; do not be afraid. I am not being tempted into conversion. I am merely admiring the craftsmanship of people in other traditions. I hope that one day, some of their congregation might admire our great thinkers, writers and musicians instead of regarding all our creativity as works of the devil."

"Amen to that, Rebecca. Maybe in your lifetime, or your daughter's, or her daughter's. These matters are beyond my understanding."

"But, father, you are our rabbi, and our people look up to you for answers to these questions."

"I am afraid that the only people who can resolve anti-Semitism are anti-Semites. When, one day, the vast image of the crucified Christ on the East window becomes a symbol for what it was, as historical fact, then an answer might be forthcoming, and our future might be more assured."

"What do you mean? What is this symbol?"

"Not so much a symbol, more a testifiable fact, Rebecca. Christ was a rebellious Jew killed by anti-Semitic Romans."

Rebecca remembered that their uncle had shouted such a thing in the town from which they had fled when she was a child. They had never seen him again after his arrest for blasphemy.

"I wish we had a beautiful window – I would promise not to see it as a manifestation of the divine."

"I'm afraid that the window in our house was smashed last night."

"Are we going to have to leave again?" Rebecca asked.

# THE MODEL EMPLOYEES

John was having "health issues". He was not sure how to describe them when questioned by his employer, but he knew that he was regarded as a hypochondriac or, worse, a skiver. Nonetheless, he was certain that it was not his imagination that generated the chest pains that he had been enduring recently.

His wife was more understanding because she had witnessed his inability to complete a short walk up the hill without stopping a couple of times to what she described as "just to catch his breath". Of course, it did not feel it was a breathing problem to him. The palpitations were more like "chest drumming" or "limb numbing". But what's in a name? He just found himself stopping for half a minute before his heartbeat slowed so he could continue climbing the hill.

The fact that the job was tediously easy did not help. "Health issues" aside, his boss, Brian, knew that anyone – including a skiver – could fulfil the basic requirements of the work. By contrast, Brian regarded his own job as so difficult that he felt it necessary to explain this repetitively to John and his colleagues. "You are all so fortunate that you have me running the ship". Of course, there was no "ship" – just a dingy office processing paper-based invoices and placing their contents onto the company network via a set of very old, worn-out keyboards with irregular connections to the network.

"You've not finished this set," Brian accused him of

missing out a whole page.

"Wasn't I entering those just as the network connection broke down?" he asked.

"I think it was when you were taking a rest because you said you weren't feeling too good. If the job is becoming too hard, I can have a word with Human Resources about bringing in a youngster to take your place."

Even when he was not suffering any "health issues", his boss could pretend that they were enough to call in Human Resources.

"Just because the company cannot be bothered to replace these old machines does not mean that Human Resources should be assessing my competence on them."

It was getting late, and John knew the final set needed inputting before the end of the day. He moved over to the most reliable keyboard in the hope that it would stay online long enough for him to complete that week's record. Brian could not be bothered to hang around to watch John's work. He wanted to get home before the traffic built up. If he returned to work after the weekend and discovered that the record had not been completed, he reckoned that this would be sufficient reason to give John his marching orders and bring in one of those young girls whom Brian would much prefer to look at.

After he had finished the last page, John stayed to check that the data had successfully transferred. Once this was confirmed, he prepared to leave the office. There was no one else in the building except Jason, the security guard, whose sole qualification for holding this role was that he was Brian's nephew.

John always came up to the office in the lift but walked down the four flights of stairs when leaving. It was a ritual that convinced him that he was still fit and well (managing four flights!) without taxing his heart. He told Brian that he always managed the stairs on foot and Brian replied that he could do the same.

The energy-saving evening lighting had come on automatically, so the stairwell was only lit by the emergency bulbs. As he rounded the second-floor flight, he nearly tripped over Brian lying at the top of the final staircase.

"Brian! Can you hear me?"

Brian was not moving. John shouted as loudly as he could. "Jason! Jason! Get up here quick!"

The fat lad sauntered up the stairs, moaning that he was not paid to sort out stairwell problems. "My job is watching the front door. What do you want?" he called back.

"It's your uncle. I think he's had a stroke or a heart attack. Call an ambulance."

Jason obviously did not believe what he was being told. Either it was some sort of test to see if he would abandon his front door duties, or a joke being played by his not-very-funny uncle. The boy eventually reached John, who was trying to revive Brian by pumping his chest.

"That's not how to do it," Jason called, having just completed his compulsory first aid training. He bent down, evidently awaiting his uncle to sit up and congratulate him on correcting John's attempts at revival. It was only after about twenty seconds of pressing his uncle's chest that it occurred to Jason that, maybe, John's order to call the ambulance was serious.

Jason stood up, sweating. "Oh my God! This is bad!" He turned to run down the stairs, tripped, and plunged headfirst down the stairwell.

John peered down into the darkness. "Jason, are you alright?" The silence told him that he now had two emergencies on his hands. He had to get to the phones at the front desk as a priority but knew not to follow Jason's example. He carefully felt his way down the final staircase, stepping over the unconscious Jason, lying across the bottom two steps.

At the reception desk, he grabbed one of the phone receivers and dialled 999. Nothing happened.

"Damn! This must be an internal phone. Perhaps I need to press 0 to get an outside line."

That did not work, the phone just gave a long whistling sound. He moved to another receiver. This seemed to be an outside line as it emitted a 'ready' signal. He dialled 999.

"Which service do you require?"

"Ambulance."

"Where are you."

John could not think of the address, so he just said the name of the employer.

"Where are you calling from, sir."

"The front desk. I've two men unconscious. I think one has had a heart attack, and the other one has fallen down the stairs."

"Thank you, sir. But can you be more specific as to your location?"

John thought for a moment, then spotted a set of business cards on the desk with the company address printed at the top. While he was waiting for the ambulance, John sat Jason up because he was lying almost upside down. Once he manoeuvred Jason the right way up, the boy appeared to be breathing normally. So, John ran up the stairs to check on Brian.

The police arrived just before the ambulance. The front door was opened by a newly revived, although stunned, Jason.

"Where are the casualties?" they asked. Jason was still confused after his fall and was unsure what the police were asking. When the paramedics ran in, looking for the heart attack victim, they found both at the top of the stairs.

# JACKPOTS

Jack was astonished. His wife, Jill, received the call and passed on the message breathlessly. "You won't believe it, my love, but that was the Lottery people. They wanted to tell us. You have just won the grand final jackpot!!"

Jack jumped off his chair with excitement. "I don't believe it! Are you sure that it's not a hoax?"

"It was Angela Amiss, the celebrity presenter. She said to check your bank account. The money will have gone in now."

Jack grabbed his laptop and quickly went through the password section. He was so excited that he got it wrong the first time. Jill told him to calm down. She sat beside him, massaging his shoulders, helping him to concentrate. The screen lit up; they both held their breath.  And there it was. The credit balance, normally just a couple of hundred pounds, showed the account now stood at over five million!

Jack's mobile phone buzzed. He picked it up and promptly dropped it with excitement. Jill retrieved it and handed it over. He listened to the voice at the other end. Nodding and saying "yes" half a dozen times, he eventually put the mobile down and spoke to Jill.

"That was Angela Amiss. She suggested that we talk with her manager about containing the publicity. She also said they could advise about managing so much money. She wanted to know if we were happy to meet her and her film crew as the public announcement was being made. I just agreed to everything."

"Very good," Jill replied. "We could use all their help. They know far more about all this. Where are we going to meet them?"

"She offered to bring her team to our house. We might prefer that rather than having to go to the tv studio tomorrow."

There was a lot to organise before the tv crew arrived. Jack phoned their two grown-up children who, unsurprisingly, believed this was a scam. But when he transferred fifty thousand pounds into each of their accounts, they started to celebrate. Jill contacted her Engineering Manager to explain why she would be missing the test of the new hyperlink rocket navigation system that she oversaw. He moaned, "Missus Pots, you are the expert. the Minister would want you there."

He needed reassurance. She spoke calmly saying; "The Minister only wants you, Director. You're in charge. I'm just a technician. The test will all go smoothly: you don't need me there."

--

Angela Amiss arrived with a flurry of photographers. Jack had dressed in his best suit and Jill squeezed into a dress she had last worn at a party a decade ago. The interview went off without a hitch although Jack was curious about two men in dark suits who stood apart from the film crew. They seemed to be paying close attention to Jill and, after the interview, approached her while Angela was shaking Jack's hand and bidding him a fond farewell.

"Are those two your money management people?" he asked Angela.

She shook her head. "I've no idea who they are."

Jill was listening to the men and seemed to be concentrating. Then, they turned abruptly and walked out of the house without another word. Jack shuffled his way around the film crew to talk to Jill.

"Who were they?" he asked. Jill put her finger up to her lips. "Shhh. I'll tell you later."

--

They were alone and Jill whispered, "I passed on some information from work to those men. They said that they hoped we enjoy our reward."

Jack frowned. "I thought it was strange as I've never bought a lottery ticket."

# SPEECH

"Everyone knows I am accustomed to public speaking."

Giovanni drew himself up to his full height and focused his eyes upon listeners whom he could not see. He always projected his voice so that anyone sitting at the farthest reaches of an auditorium would be able to hear his every word.

"In many ways, I have become something of a cliché amongst storytellers. I am told that my tales are predictable because they always end with a twist. But today I am going to surprise you with a story that is the opposite of inventive. I shall lay before you an account that more exactly mirrors reality than anything I have ever written."

He waited to bring more gravity to his voice. The pause was intended to heighten tension and ensure that any temptation amongst listeners to interrupt, to cough, to fail to follow his flow would be expunged, erased, eviscerated.

There was silence. He took two deep breaths, then resumed.

"Anna was the most fascinating girl. Years ago, you will remember how powerful an effect she had upon boys of our age. Not only young boys, I hasten to add, but also grown men whose eyes and hearts would be drawn towards her as she glided into a room or was viewed walking nonchalantly down the street.

Some of you were my competitors in the desperate struggle to win her over. The unfortunate skirmishes of youth that often set us apart were entirely generated by her presence. If she had lived in another land, many of those who became my enemies would have remained my friends. But the old cliché about all being fair in love and war seems inadequate to explain how we behaved to one another in Anna's presence and even when she was nowhere to be seen.

I don't know how many of you really knew Anna's father. He was a bull of a man, dominating his poor wife but treating Anna like a fairy. He always wanted her dressed up in dainty clothes to parade before them as the family made its way to the Sunday church service. This was the weekly show. This was his demonstration of how he thought a great, aristocratic family might walk with pride through the peasantry, contrasting their dignity and grace with the uncouth townsfolk whom he believed looked up to them. With this upbringing, you would expect Anna to have been a spoilt brat. But nothing could be further from the truth.

When, at last, I managed to speak with Anna alone, she showed not the slightest hint of haughtiness. Quite the contrary, she saw herself as a studious young girl who had to put up with the constant attentions of the boys and men of the town whilst coping with the snobbery and stupidity of her oppressive father who had only been a corporal in the army. She spoke about how much of her time was spent supporting her mother whose marriage had become a nightmare. I listened to her description of home life. It was not a pretty tale.

She asked me about what I liked most about life. This was a strange request. She did not ask about what I wanted to do or to become. She asked about life as a whole. Did I want to travel? Did I have any great ambitions? Maybe these would have been easy-to-answer questions. But to ask about life … not just mine … about life itself. Anna had a way of opening out conversations from the specific to the general. But I was too clumsy and only managed to describe what I liked about my life at that time, the specific activities that interested me as a young man.

Some of you were in the same karate team that I captained. It was a self-defence discipline with a view to controlling and guiding the aggressive instincts of any young man. Despite being promoted by the coach, I knew that some of you were far better practitioners, certainly more able to harness your powers and impose a calm, meditative aura around your movements. I know only too well that mine lacked control and would require more years before I could achieve a black belt.

When Anna kissed me, I was elated. I was surprised because I honestly had no idea that this beautiful girl saw me as anything other than a boy who happened to be in the same class at school. I am sure that our relationship was innocent. Thinking back, now, I might tinge my memory with more passionate impulses. But I do not believe that they were foremost at the time. We were just close friends who felt able to unburden ourselves of our worries and concerns. For Anna, these were all focused upon her father.

Now we come to the moment that I know you would want me to describe in as much detail as I can remember. But the truth is that there is almost nothing to tell. We were walking home, talking and holding hands when her father suddenly confronted us. I had not seen him as he swung around the corner by the graveyard. He screamed something, I could not make out the words. Indeed, I do not know if they were words. And he seized Anna by the throat and thrust her aside. Then he turned on me and swung his fist at my head. I ducked and he screamed again. Before he could hit me with his next swing, I jabbed him just to push him away. I did not aim at his throat but as he ducked towards me, that is where my knuckle struck him.

I know that Anna does not believe that I was using my karate technique to kill her father. But that is how the judge saw it."

Giovanni sat down and looked at the cell's blank walls and hoped that Anna and her mum might now enjoy what they most like about life.

# NARCISSUS

Revolutions start at home. The only revolution in which I was involved began in my niece's bedroom. You will not remember what it was like to live in a country dominated by out-of-control gangs. Their constant fighting over who owned the money-making flower fields, left dozens of young men dead every month. People from other nations no longer visited our lovely country, afraid of being caught up in the violence. At the United Nations, we were described as a Narci State.

It was not even in our country that the cream from the narcissus plant was found to arrest the process of skin ageing. The production of the competing brands "Celestial Skin" and "Fair Forever" was legal and not subject to any trade restrictions. The Fantasy Flesh beauty products were advertised widely and became the first choice of gifts for every teenaged boy or girl. I can recall meeting Karen, my old school friend, just before my fortieth birthday. She looked exactly as I remembered her when she was nineteen. She was shocked to see how I had aged. "Why didn't you use Fair Forever?" she asked. I just shrugged and said something non-committal like "Oh! I was never very good at choosing what to buy."

My sister was married to a Narci boss. But their daughter, my niece, had a mind of her own. Her social media presence, magnified no doubt by the reputation of her father, was where she began demonstrating online the use of a radical alternative to Fantasy Flesh products. The notion that beauty was irrevocably tied into a youthful appearance was challenged by her praising "mature magnificence" and undermining the attractions of what she termed "the expensive flights of fantasy" chasing "pathetic prettiness." Her model, at first, I did not realise it was me, her aunt, was presented as 'archetypal beauty' and my hardworking husband as the ideal "generous gentleman". The alternative that revolutionised the industry and led to the eventual demise of all Fantasy Flesh products was readily available in most countries. And where it was not, a huge irresistible demand grew to make it available – clean water (combined with non-perfumed soap).

Our country has been born again. People from across the world feel safe here. The gangs are long gone. The former narcissus fields grow vegetables and the abandoned statue of Narcissus that still stands before the Town Hall is the favourite perching spot for defecating crows. I came across an old bottle of Celestial Skin. I wonder, should I use it to retain my 'magnificently mature' appearance into old age?

# HIGH JUMP

Richard Douglas Fosbury was an American high jumper, who is considered one of the most influential athletes in the history of track and field. He won a gold medal at the 1968 Summer Olympics, revolutionising the high jump event with a "back-first" technique now known as the Fosbury flop.

I was one of the top high jumpers. Of course, this was before the novelty of leaping back-first became the norm. Being something of a traditionalist, it took me some time before I adopted this admittedly more effective approach.

Strangely, it was not the added height that persuaded me to alter my lifelong commitment to what I called my belly roll. I am ashamed to confess that the critical moment came when I saw the gleam in the eyes of young females admiring us experimenting with various forms of backflip.

I know that some regarded my late adoption of this new technique as a rather pathetic attempt by one so old to take on the athleticism of youth. But I always ignored the backbiting and envious criticism of those who, in most cases, were never contenders in their own right. Instead, even if it courted disaster, I decided to risk all in that year's competition and play the youngsters at their own game. Spurred on by the heckling, I went by the motto 'fortune favours the brave'.

In my first leap, I noticed the stir made in the crowd. But my main competitor was the brilliant world record holder. He performed a phenomenal leap that looked even more spectacular as he twisted at the apogee of his jump creating an artificially elongated shadow before the setting sun – an awe-inspiring image I shall never forget.

The challenge he set me was to break his sensational world record which would have been incredible even to think of in the days of the belly roll. But I was game to try a backflip as none of us yet knew what gravitational limitations existed in this new high jump era.

I can recall every second of my acceleration towards the famous leap. At the very moment of take-off I genuinely felt that there would be absolutely nothing to prevent my body from flying into a stratospheric realm never achieved before or since.

The death-defying descent brought me dozens of female followers, dazzled by the beauty of the magnificent elliptical arc highlighted by the sun slipping gracefully below the Southern Ocean horizon.

# THE PROOFREADER

She enjoyed her job. Celebrated authors, as well as a few newcomers, regularly sent her their scripts to proofread. She was trusted as the most fanatically precise enforcer of the accepted rules of grammar and syntax. Nothing escaped her view of how a sentence should best be structured, how occasional slips into the passive when the active verb would be more appropriate, how a temptation to overkill with prepositions or adverbs obscured meaning, and how punctuation errors could throw the entire emphasis away from the author's obvious intention.

She accepted poor pay as she knew that she was not the creator of the stories, only their first assessor. From what she gleaned from the authors themselves, they rarely enjoyed a substantial income unless they were one of the half dozen bestsellers who asked for her help. Apart from poor spelling that these famous few appeared to demonstrate more than the youthful newcomers, they rarely required much alteration as many of their sentences and paragraphs had been either checked or even composed by artificial intelligence software.

Her favourite authors were the newcomers. They seemed less offended when she suggested alterations to their texts: some even welcomed her changes and acknowledged that they represented significant improvements! There was one renowned author (we will not say who he was) who regularly challenged her suggestions. "That is not what I meant!" he would harass her on the phone. "I cannot see why you would think that your word order was an improvement. It fails to retain the emphasis at the end of the paragraph." Her quietly pointing out that it retained the emphasis whilst correcting a glaring punctuation error would only be accepted when his publisher pointed out that she was right.

When her husband suggested that she might like to write herself, she shook her head. "I am not imaginative. Some of these writers have such a way with words: I cannot possibly stand beside them. Some are giants of the literary establishment. I would not even know what to write about."

Her husband was a firm supporter, he loved their children, he loved her. He was a constant breadwinner, and, with his support, she knew that her low income was not important for the family budget. "You should write about what you know," he said. "It cannot do any harm just to see how it feels to be the creator rather than the checker."

"But what do I know about? There are hundreds, maybe thousands, of books by women describing their lives as home makers. There are even more that imagine themselves in more passionate relationships that attract readers who just want to identify with a romantic heroine. I really do not want to write like that. It just isn't who I am."

"But, darling, you have another life that is quite unlike any others. Think of your work. Think of all the contact you have with celebrated authors as well as with many youngsters who are not yet famous. Couldn't you write about your experience as a proofreader?"

She thought the idea almost ridiculous. Who on earth would want to read about the meticulous procedures she went through checking other people's texts? Who else would be interested in syntactic structures in the English language and how they could alter the meaning of texts supplied in translated form from other languages?

Her little book, that her husband offered to proofread as a joke, was a sensation. Without revealing the names of the authors, readers tried to guess to whom she was referring when seeming to poke fun at their ignorance of their own language. Newspaper critics offered their opinions, but she steadfastly refused to say whether the book referred to specific authors or whether she was writing a fictional account of the life of a proofreader. Her publisher was pressing her for a second book. "If the next one sells like your first, you will be earning more than any of those for whom you've been proofreading!"

"I hope so," she said, "because most have declared they will never have me as their proofreader again."

# BLACK AND WHITE

*What colour was Schrödinger's cat?*

Judith Bat-Merari had always been good at chess. Aged seven she could beat her father, her uncle, and even the President of the town's chess club. It did not matter whether she was playing black or white, her unerring sense of when to launch an attack was later confirmed as the choice of the yet-to-be-invented chess supercomputers.

In an article written about Judith as a teenager, she responded to a question about how she felt when thrown into important matches.

"Do you ever feel nervous?" Cyrus Holofernes had asked. Cyrus was a champion and often spoke about the irrelevance of the separation between the sexes, "Chess is chess irrespective of the player's genitals" was one of his most cited sayings. Judith knew about his celebrity and answered: "I think I might feel nervous if I had to play against you."

The article began with an irrelevant, although now pertinent, sentence or two about Cyrus's political opinions and why he believed that military men or women were the best leaders. Then it droned on about Judith's boredom at school with teachers who did not want to be there, the interference of having to play sports when all Judith wanted was to study chess positions and her visceral fear of losing a game. It was only this last item that caught the attention of later readers, after Judith's notoriety was at its height.

Nobody can now verify if the words she is quoted as

having used were totally accurate. But they seem relevant when considering how Judith evolved as a player and human being. "There are critical moments in any chess game when you are playing against a strong player. It is as if time stands still, and you float high above the board. You look down and see all the possible future patterns. You feel invisible eyes are watching you. Your decision about the next move is more important than anything you have ever done or are likely to do. You sense that your opponent is trying to divert you from a true path. They are driven by diabolical forces that it is your destiny to defeat. And then you make your move."

Judith was the most successful top board, playing for her country a dozen times. We all believed she was on a path eventually to challenge for the world title. Her extraordinary run of games where she was only held to a draw on five occasions during a run of nearly one hundred victories has never been equaled. There is a police report that records that both Judith and Cyrus were staying in the same hotel whilst she was on tour with the national team. Nothing more is reported until Cyrus's body was found in his room beside a chessboard whose pieces had been left with black clearly mating the white king. Judith had disappeared and no one has seen her since.

Many theories were created about what might or might not have happened in Cyrus's room that night. There were a few signs that Judith had been there, two glasses of water beside the board, the bloody cheese wire used to decapitate Cyrus had come from a cheese and wine set from Judith's room. But most dispute between commentators revolved around who was playing black, and who was losing as white. Cyrus Hollofernes was a grandmaster whose playing style was very different from Judith's. He enjoyed military-style attack manoeuvres that attempted to beat down the opponent, often capturing many pieces before finalising the game with an overwhelming force. Judith's game was more subtle, building up tiny positional advantages and preferring activity above material gain. As both queens, all the rooks and most of the bishops were still on the board at the moment of checkmate, some experts have argued that Cyrus was white and had been outplayed by Judith before he had even had a chance to start taking her pieces. On the other hand, she may have been shocked by an early defeat before she had the chance to reach that point where time stood still.

Cyrus Hollofernes' political views had become more extreme by the time of his beheading. It is possible that Judith regarded their presence together in a room as a unique opportunity to cut short the intrigues and campaigns in which he was involved. Some have ventured that Cyrus may have made unwanted advances towards the attractive woman in his room and when rebuffed had sought to overpower her physically. Her defensive moves may have knocked him out cold and her decision to kill him was a logical attempt to forestall what was likely to occur once he regained consciousness.

There are those who seek to defend Judith and others who seek to assert Cyrus's innocence. But, unlike chess, it seems that nothing here is clearly black or white.

# THE PERFECT PRINCIPLES OF ART

Pilgrim unburdened himself to his wife. "It's impossible to make any headway in the organisation unless you are an accredited Adept."

"How can you achieve that?" Sally asked.

"I've no idea but I'm sure the director has already decided that I can never join the élite."

Pilgrim had become accustomed to the director's incomprehensible orders. He knew that she was an Adept. "I suppose you're a Senior Adept," he had asked the week before. Janice's response was precisely what any average Extra would expect from a director.

"Results, Pilgrim. That is all that matters. My seniority is irrelevant. Your part is as important as the highest paid star. Everything we do, we do here at this gym. We have no need for expensive film sets. Adept philosophy is Stoic."

Pilgrim had no idea about philosophy. But he understood he would be paid for acting out the part set for him. So, he dutifully carried out press-ups on the polished gym floor. He managed twenty before starting to feel tired. "That's enough!" Janice called. Pilgrim was relieved.

It was not until the following week, after Pilgrim had left the set and was working at the company spaceport as a temporary security guard, that Sally called.

"You must REALLY like working with that woman!" she shouted. Pilgrim had no idea of what he was being accused. "What woman?"

"Don't play the innocent with me. Wait till you get

home!" and she had rung off.

The 3-d video of his press-ups had been carefully spliced into making it appear that Janice was beneath his exertions, naked, sultry, and thoroughly enjoying the experience. Sally, disbelieving all his protestations of innocence, had walked out. Her suitcase had already been packed and her visa and travel ticket stamped, ready for departure from the spaceport where he had just been working.

Pilgrim was furious and stormed into the studio to get hold of Janice and her Adept crew. They had been prepared to destroy his marriage just to make money from a pornographic film. He threw open the doors, but the place was silent. He surveyed the gym where he had performed but it smelled musty and disused. His footsteps echoed around the empty space as he looked for a door into an office or reception area. But the only door was the one he had just entered from the street.

Cursing how he had been tricked and how quickly the Adept gang had packed up and left, he was determined to track down Janice (or whoever she really was) and confront her with the wrongs he had suffered. Above all, he wanted to extract a confession that could be played back to Sally to persuade her to come back home.

There were no obvious clues where he should search but he remembered Janice referring to something called Stoic philosophy. He had no idea what this meant: so, he looked it up on the Internet. His mobile phone described a Roman, Marcus Aurelius, who was credited with practising this philosophy.

It took a couple of days before he realised that reading snippets from various reference books brought him no nearer understanding Stoic philosophy, nor to where Janice and her crew may have disappeared.

Feeling dejected, he decided to track down his wife and appeal to her with an honest account of what had happened. He knew that although Sally was unlikely to believe him, he would at least have the satisfaction of having presented the truth. What would happen afterwards was nothing he could influence. He would simply resign himself to whatever the world had in store for him.

At the spaceport, he had a shrewd idea where Sally would fly to. The Rejected Refuge, as it was known, welcomed women who had been abused or abandoned by their partner. He had no idea if he would be allowed to disembark, but he bought a ticket at the Adept Flight Desk.

Take-off was in darkness, and he fell asleep. When he woke up, the flight was progressing smoothly, and the flight staff were distributing beverages and reading material. "We apologise that the video screens are not functioning on this flight," the chief steward announced, "but we hope that the Adept Reading Books will be of interest."

Pilgrim groaned. The last thing he wanted was to study more literature after wasting the past days researching the elusive Marcus Aurelius in the hope of discovering where Janice's Adept gang had hidden themselves.

He opened the book handed to him along with the unappetising, cold pie that was meant to make his journey less gruelling. He took one bite and discarded the tasteless lump of dough stuffed with artificial protein filler. He glanced at the book, 'Meditations by Marcus Aurelius' and opened it at random at Book IV.

Let no act be done without a purpose, nor otherwise than according to the perfect principles of art.

Pilgrim grimaced. He had read enough in the previous couple of days to know what Stoic "art" consisted of. In his childhood, he had been told it would have been described as "righteous living." He reflected upon how he had been surviving and, in all honesty, did not believe that old Marcus Aurelius would have had many complaints about his temperate existence. He was a quiet vegetarian, he always provided for Sally and never consorted with crooks, low-lifes and prostitutes. He rarely lost his temper and tended to work as an obedient servant for whoever employed him. He concluded that his acts had followed "the perfect principles of art" as best he could manage. But that had not protected him against those who wished to exploit him.

Upon landing, Pilgrim walked through Control without anyone asking him the purpose of his visit. He sat in one of the ready-taxis and told the robot driver that he wanted to find his wife, Sally. "No problem, sir," the crackly voice from the front intoned. The vehicle whizzed through the traffic.

It broke down ten minutes away from the Aurelius Hotel. Pilgrim sighed, paid the driver without protest, and set off, uncomplaining, to walk the last mile. At the reception desk, the lady clerk smiled and asked him to sit at the bar. She said: "Your wife will be along soon."

Pilgrim was puzzled. How did the clerk know about Sally? She pointed to the bar area, and he reluctantly wandered over. But he was confronted by a large man leaving the bar, apparently worse for wear after too much alcohol. The drunk swung at him, but his fist was too high. Pilgrim could see that the man was not in control of his actions so guided him carefully over to the receptionist. "I think this guest might benefit from a night's sleep. Perhaps one of your porters could take him to his room."

Pilgrim turned away from the receptionist and finally arrived at the bar. He did not like the room. It was surrounded by screens that projected moving images without accompanying sound. It was as if these were old silent films being haphazardly displayed to anyone who happened to be passing. He was not paying much attention to what was being shown when the clerk gave a little cough behind him.

"Excuse me, sir, but is that you on the film?"

He spun around just in time to see the end of the clip with him pressing down upon Janice.

"You were very good. Are you a professional actor?" She asked.

Suddenly Sally appeared at the reception desk and shouted: "No, he isn't acting. But he is a professional!"

He leapt up and ran towards the desk, but Sally disappeared down the corridor. He ran after her, but she must have got into one of the two elevators. He watched the indicators to gauge to which floor they were headed. One went down to the basement, and one shot up to the top floor. He guessed she would have gone up as the basement was just for the swimming pool – and Sally could not swim.

The elevator arrived from the basement, and he jumped in pressing the button to take it to the top floor. It had already been pressed by whoever had got in from the basement. The lift door closed, and Janice spoke to him.

"We wondered when you were going to get here."

Pilgrim trembled with incomprehensible rage. "What the hell is going on?" he screamed. "What are you doing here? Why are you following Sally? Why did you make that disgusting film?"

The elevator arrived and the door opened. Sally got in and gave Janice a hug. Pilgrim stood there with his mouth wide open. "How do you two know each other?"

Janice replied. "Amazing! You've been married for how long?"

"Twelve years," Sally answered.

"And in all that time, Pilgrim, did you never suspect that

your wife was an Adept?”

“What has this got to do with that pornographic film?”

“There is no film: that was a private video especially prepared for your viewing.”

“But why? What possible motive could you have for scaring me and threatening my marriage?”

“There’s never been a threat,” Sally intervened. “Once you decided to come and find me here, we knew that you could only have accomplished that by being a Stoic.”

Pilgrim’s heart was beating too fast. He stopped still for a moment, then bent over whilst catching his breath. Both women came to him, anxious that he was not suffering some kind of seizure or heart attack. After a minute he stood up and took a deep breath.

“I’m sorry, darling,” Sally apologised. “Everyone who is to become an Adept must pass through the test.

Pilgrim nodded and started towards the luxury penthouse bedroom.

Janice entered. He followed, then firmly shut the door.

# THE BEAUTIFUL GAME

My father had been a famous striker, and my millionaire brother owned the franchise manufacturing standard leg protectors. The family expected each of us to make a mark in the world of international football.

It was not long after Rule-Free Football became the darling sport of the People that I found my unique niche. Since my dad's day, the game had evolved from the old international soccer game. Now, teams transcended mere national boundaries and had grown into the multibillion-dollar enterprises whose owners held majority shareholdings in all social and mass media outlets.

The capacity to score goals became only one of several factors that decided a team's success. The ability to inflict injury or worse upon opponent's key players was as important to ensuring victory and, more importantly, supporter popularity. The top teams featured astonishingly fast running scorers, their equally rapid parrying group and the heavyweight defending cadre whose spiked boots could grip both soft ground and opponents' legs.

With no limit upon the number of substitutes, top teams would arrive at an opponent's ground with over a hundred players, expecting at least twenty to be hospitalised in any one game. The champions in my final year as a sports correspondent maintained six home grounds, one on each continent, each with their own limb repair clinic. In my early years, I had been a referee in the children's competitions until referees and linesmen were eventually abolished in favour of the non-stop game. Following some political pressure, (of which I have said repeatedly I was unaware) I had been identified as the most attractive person to undertake the ritual interview of the winning manager. The continuous market testing of viewers found that my physical attributes were the reason why a significant number of supporters tuned into our social and mass media channels.

"What do you feel was the key to your success this year?" I asked, ensuring that the split down my skirt was directly before camera one.

"Our heavies were superb, don't you think? I can only remember a couple of occasions when enemy strikers scored."

"Next year's recruits are being drawn from right across the world. Have you any message for aspiring players that might get them noticed by your army of scouts?"

"It is their spirit scouts are watching for – not just physical ability. We need players who will give their very soul to the sport and the team."

I puffed up my chest for a prearranged camera two close-up of my cleavage.

"How can young players demonstrate their spirit?"

"That's a very good question, my dear. Only the top scouts really know the answer. But we are not just major sporting providers: we also generate vast sums for charitable causes. All players take part in the big news features showing the team's generosity to poor and disabled people around the world. Last year alone, we contributed more than any other team to African children who needed bread and water to survive."

"You know one of your opponent teams has gone on record to accuse you of poaching one of their top players. That was after he broke all viewing records by releasing a song with his own band that celebrated the sensation of scoring. He sang that it is even better than sex. How do you respond to that accusation?"

"Well, I'm willing to test that out if you are?"

I smiled demurely, giggled softly, and pursed my newly enlarged lips "Well, we'll see about that later, maybe. Meanwhile, what do you think about that player?"

"He will definitely NOT be playing for our team. We have never poached anyone … not ever!  The accusation is entirely false. We were not involved with his decision to leave their team. His off-the-field injury took place in a hotel room that had nothing to do with us. Perhaps you could interview the three women who shared his room to discover what they did together.

I smiled, nodded approvingly towards the director at this invitation to obtain yet another sporting scoop, and carried on.

"Moving forward, how do you see the coming year. What do you think will be the key features?"

"Well obviously there's the China Cup which is worth over sixty billion dollars – and we are very grateful to the Chinese government for subsidising and televising the entire competition. Then there's the American Cup, worth seventy billion dollars this year and we are grateful to the American government for its generous subsidy decided after the Chinese government announced how much it was committing to its competition. We are currently in discussion with the Brazilian government that has formed an international conglomerate with India, Russia, South Africa and the Arab Union to discover if they can provide a new International Cup worth one hundred billion dollars!"

"Well! That is exciting!" I had arranged that moment for the split in my skirt to fall wide open. "Can you tell me is there any chance of Rule-Free Football becoming the dominant sport in Europe?"

With a sad shake of his head he replied, "I am afraid that so many of their public are quite old fashioned and cling on to the ancient game of soccer. They still play with referees!"

I shook my head, letting my long, blonde wig reflect the spotlight across at camera three.

"Also, that backward continent has not got the resources to fund our great sport. They have been left behind. We are waiting for them to catch up. Your network might tell us when that will be as your market research team could be the first to detect a change in mood amongst spectators."

He raised his hands in mock disbelief. "Can you understand this? My scout in Rome reported that many were still more concerned with bread than circuses!"

I took in a huge breath, puffing out my breasts, so I could let out a long, contemptuous laugh.

He joined in and exclaimed: "Oh! We do have such a beautiful game!"

# TRANSMIGRATION

It was an unexpected privilege to be asked to interview Kwan Yin. Since her withdrawal from the spotlight of the world's media, she had shunned contact with journalists like me. So, I was intrigued as to the reason why I had been invited to visit her in the Buddhist community at the foothills of the Himalayas.

On my way, I re-read many of the articles about the most famous woman on the planet. Her mysterious birth was dated from the day that the monks found her deposited on their doorstep and the failure of subsequent investigators to gain even a clue as to who her parents might be. I read about her sheltered childhood and precocious academic abilities that were overshadowed by her amazing physical growth into the seven-foot giantess who could outrun any male. There were plenty of photographs that covered the extraordinary Delhi Olympic Games where she was granted special dispensation to compete in the men's events. Everyone knows about her exploits there: her breaking of the 9 second 100 metres barrier, her winning gold at the long jump and her unbelievable run finishing nearly a mile ahead of the nearest marathon runner. Drug testing found her totally "clean" and she spoke humbly about her strictly vegetarian diet, her hours of meditation before any event and the unusually slow pulse rate to which so-called experts attributed her achievements.

It was only two years later that it was realised that the

breakthroughs in mathematics which promoted the Indian sub-continent into its current leadership role were driven by her work. Publishing her findings under a pseudonym, she tried to avoid the adulation that she saw would be heaped upon her yet again. As a young science reporter, I had asked her how she had come to see through the complex problems that had foxed brilliant minds for generations. Her reply that was printed in most newspapers (the only scoop I have ever had!) was frightening in its simplicity. "I view the problem; I meditate upon why it is problematic; I see why it is no problem when viewed from afar; I come closer and write down the solution as I see it."

Her withdrawal back into the Himalayan Sangha at the age of thirty was frustrating for the media hungry for more information about Kwan Yin. But the community protected her privacy, and it was only twenty-five years later that she agreed to an interview and specified that she would only speak to me. Her appearance was a shock. Still standing a full head and shoulders taller than me, she gracefully shook my hand and asked me to sit beside her. Her hair was still jet black and hung down to her waist, just as it had done as she streaked across the racetrack thirty years before. She smiled and I was disorientated for a moment as she seemed to me to be exactly as I remembered her when she had described her method for solving mathematics problems.

"So, what have you been doing with yourself since I last saw you?" I asked in a weak attempt to open the conversation.

She surveyed me quietly. "My first duties were to care for my children."

"You have children?!" I was so surprised that I nearly leapt from my seat.

"Yes, I have twin boys."

"And are they here in the sangha?"

"No. They prefer to keep quiet about their mother; so, you may not know them. But one went into business and is already one of the wealthiest men in India. The other is a leading practitioner of martial arts. I am most proud of them. But now they have gone. Our children are only on loan and mine have now happily returned to the world."

"Have you continued with your meditation? Have you gained any further insights that you might share?"

She suddenly looked sad. "I feel I have failed in this life," she intoned. "I have not attained bodhi and now believe that this may not be possible."

I immediately realised that Kwan Yin's aspirations towards enlightenment had drained her of much energy. I felt that she perhaps wanted some sort of encouragement from me – a mere journalist but an 'outsider' who may be able to say things that those within her community might not.

"I thought that Buddha only achieved enlightenment after he felt that this might not be possible. Perhaps you are at that stage in your pathway and that nirvana is still attainable. After all, it was for him."

Her head dropped. "It is that achievement for which we all long, the escape from the eternal return, the reincarnations from which we desire a way out. But I now know that my soul will transmigrate and, indeed, I do not believe that any souls have ever escaped."

"Surely you cannot believe that. Buddha himself showed us that this is possible."

"Unfortunately, that is not true."

"I don't understand. How could you know that his great soul did not escape and transmigrate?"

"How do you think?" she said as she quietly wept.

Also by Ray Kohn


A Jewish Odyssey


Jewish Tales Untold

9 781068 705724